Peter & the WOLF

Based on original illustrations
by Bono

Welcome, readers! Gavin Flyday here.
I'm your Master of Ceremonies, MC Superfly – some
say the Winged Wonder, a few have said Fly-by-night.
Someone even tried to swat me... Whatever, it doesn't matter.
Think of me as your trusty narrator and navigator. I'll be whizzing
around this book, taking off, dropping by. Keep an eye out
for me – you'll never know which page I may land on.

But it's not all about me, unfortunately. In fact, this story originates
from the symphonic fairytale *Peter and the Wolf*, written by Russian composer
Sergei Prokofiev (say it with me, **PRUH-KOFF-EE-EFF**) back in 1936.
His masterpiece showcased the orchestra to children, with each character
represented by a different musical instrument. Ingenious! This story
encourages us to be brave and face our fears, even in the darkest of times.
But our story has a twist to the tale that you won't see coming...

Now you're going to have to be brave. There is a deep, dark forest to
explore, shadowy figures lurking inside, and a hungry wolf
to watch out for. I'll be by your side, but don't worry,
this is your adventure...

And remember, there is nothing to be afraid of.

Yours truly,

Gavin Flyday

Beware, for wolves come in many disguises.

 *O*nce upon a time, there was a boy called **Peter**.

He lived with his grandfather in a
cottage, with a garden surrounded
by a high stone wall.

Outside the wall there was a meadow
with a pond and a tall tree.

Beyond the meadow was a

deep, dark forest.

Let me introduce you to

the characters in our story...

There is a **bird**,
light and delicate
with feathers of silk.

A **pussycat**.

She is smooth but
greedy and vain.

A silly **duck** with a
broad bill and large
webbed feet.

There is a
big grey wolf
with sharp teeth and
sharp claws, who is
always **hungry**.

There are **hunters**
searching the woods
for wolves, firing
their **shotguns**.

There is wise
old **Grandfather**.
Now he worries about
Peter **all** the time.

 And, of course,
there is **Peter**.

Now this is where the story begins.

Early one morning when Peter walked

out of the house, he opened the gate...

...and went into the big green meadow.

On a branch of a tall tree sat the pretty little bird.

All is quiet and beautiful this morning,
she said gently.

The bird was Peter's friend.

Peter made his own slingshot. He started playing
and the bird joined in.

Then Peter had an *idea*.

He'd seen something in his mother's
old bedroom that would be **perfect**.

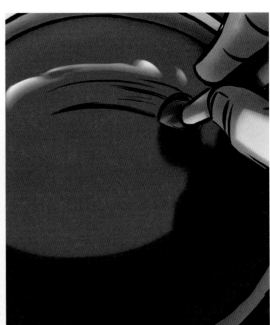
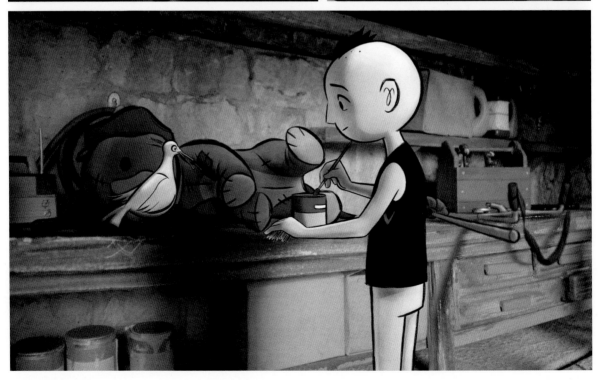

Just then, the silly duck waddled up.

She was glad the gate had been left open,
as there was a deep pond in the meadow,
and she wanted to swim.

Seeing the duck, the bird
flew down and sat next to her.

The bird, who was very sweet, said,

What kind of a bird are **you** if you **can't fly**?

What kind of a bird are **you**,

the duck said snappily, if you **can't swim**?

And with that, she hurriedly dived into the pond.

All of this led to an argument.

They **argued** and **argued**...

The duck as she splashed around in the water,

the bird flying **this** way and **that**.

Just then, something caught Peter's eye.

Pussycat was stalking through the tall grass.

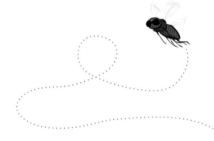

She thought to herself,
Hmmm... that bird
is busy arguing.

I can probably
get her now.

And on velvet paws, she crept ever **closer**.

Look out! shouted Peter.

The bird quickly flew into the tree.

The duck **quacked angrily** from the middle of the pond.

Pussycat walked **round** and **round**,

looking up at the bird and thinking,

Hmmm... is it worth climbing so high, I wonder?

By the time I get there, she'll have flown away.

Here comes Grandfather.

He never liked Peter to go out into the meadow.

It's not really the place for **you**
Grandson, he said gravely.

You don't know what's out there.

Wolves... and **worse**. It's dangerous.

Peter — Stay — Put.

Peter said nothing.

Of course Peter wasn't afraid of wolves,
but then he couldn't really argue
with his grandfather.

Peter was bored.

He decided to
creep outside.

Go back to the house, said Grandfather.

Then he locked the gate securely.

No sooner had Peter gone upstairs
than a **big grey wolf** came
out of the dark forest.

Pussycat turned and **saw** the wolf.

In a twinkle,
she had scarpered
up the tree.

The duck **quacked hysterically**.

But in her panic, foolishly **jumped** out of the pond.

The wolf saw the duck – it went for her like a **shot**.
And no matter how **hard** or how **fast** the duck
tried to run, she could not escape.

The wolf came in hot pursuit, nearer and nearer,

catching up,

catching up.

Then the wolf got the duck
and swallowed her **hungrily**

in one
enormous
gulp.

NOW... this is how things stood.

Pussycat was up a tree, sitting on one branch.

The bird was in the same tree, on another branch.

But not **too close** to Pussycat.

There was no great affection between them.

The wolf walked **round** and **round** beneath the tree, staring at both of them with greedy eyes.

Licking its lips.

Peter saw it all.

He thought, So the wolf wants to catch them,
but not if I catch the wolf **first**!

I'll trap the wolf. Yes.

I'm not afraid of the **big bad WOLf.**

So Peter found a strong rope, which he wrapped

round and round until he made a lasso.

He slipped it through his fingers
and tried one or two quick throws.

Peter went out noiselessly. He heaved himself up onto the
stone wall and reached the nearest branch of the tree.
Silently, he **climbed** into the tree.

Peter whispered to the bird, Be a good little Birdie.

Fly down and tease the wolf a bit.

Not too close. Just enough to keep

it busy for a moment or two.

The bird obeyed and fluttered overhead,
almost touching the wolf.

The wolf leapt upwards, snapping
its **huge sharp teeth**.

Peter climbed down and followed them into the forest.

Ever so gently, Peter slipped the rope...

...over the **wolf's tail**.

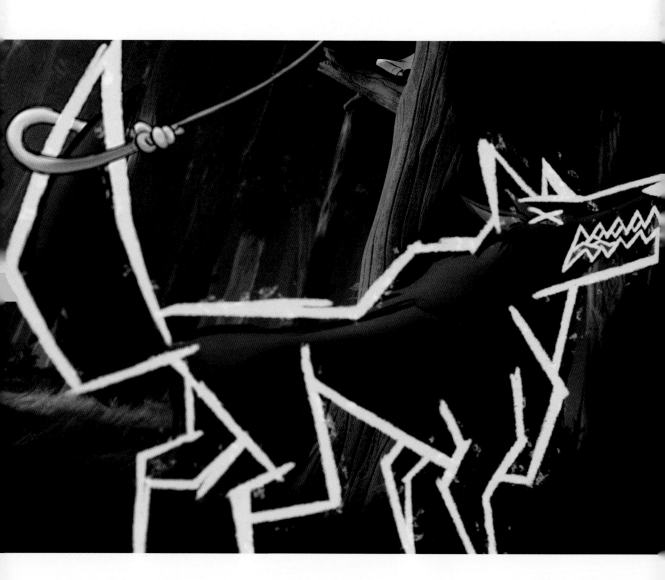

Then he pulled the rope with **all his might**.

Caught by the tail, the wolf went **berserk**.

It was jumping **WiLdLy**, trying to escape.

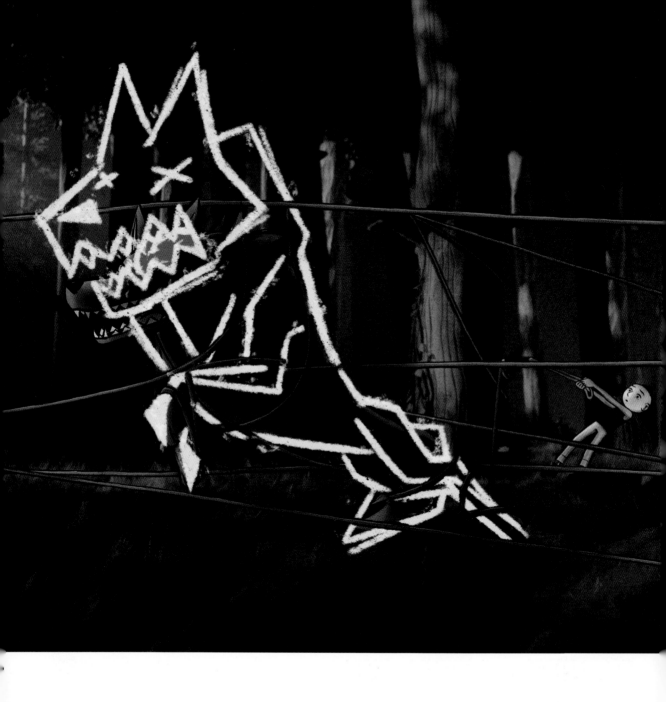

Then Peter tied his end of the rope to the tree.

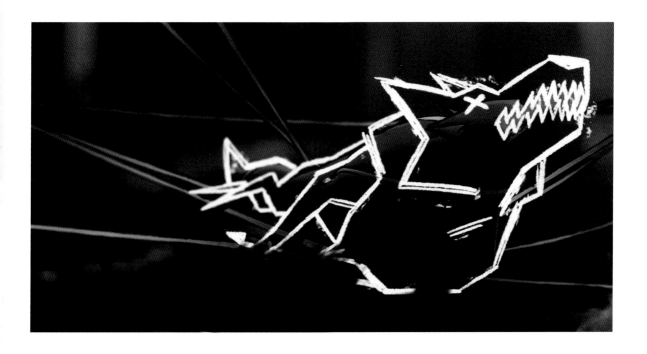

The more the wolf struggled, the **tighter** the rope became.

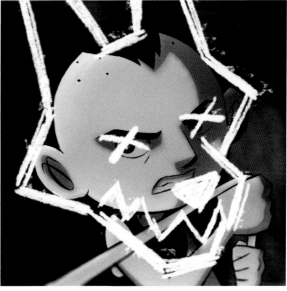

Then three young pups
came out of the shadows.

They were looking for their mother.

The hunters came striding into the
woods on the trail of the wolf.

Their shotguns **poised** and **ready**.

Grandfather appeared from the darkness.

What do we do? said Peter.

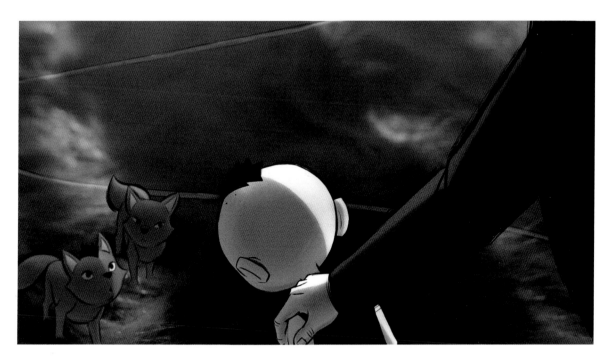

Shhh... said Grandfather.

Wolves come in many disguises.

Stop shooting! Peter shouted.

But the hunters couldn't hear him.

Again, he shouted,

Stop! Put away your guns!

Birdie and I have caught the wolf.

BANG!

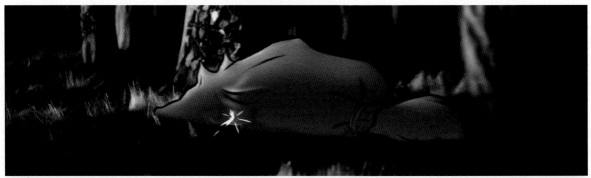

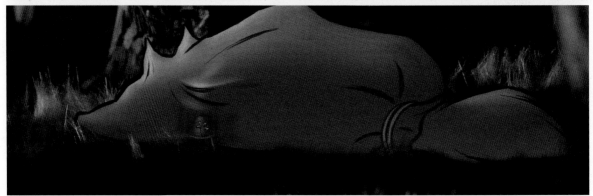

The hunters jumped for joy.

 But had they

really caught the wolf?

They boasted but they never thought...

...to look closely at the wolf in the sack.

And then came the **Victory Parade**...

...Peter in front, followed by the hunters leading the wolf.

And at the back of the parade, Pussycat and Grandfather.

Now, **nothing** is ever the way they say it is.

Before the hunters arrived...

...Peter and Grandfather had **tricked** them.

What the hunters thought was the wolf,

was **not a wolf** at all.

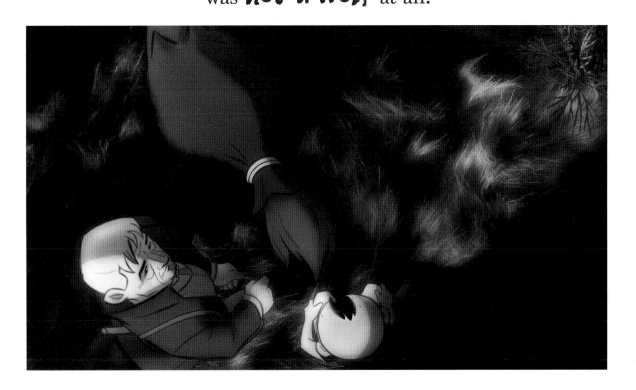

The next day was the best day, and Peter felt **less afraid**.

Birdie was quite pleased with herself.

Now, this is where the story ends.

Are the **loved ones** we've lost ever really gone?

If you listen carefully, you might just **hear their call**.

This reimagined version of *Peter and the Wolf* was originally developed by Gavin Friday and Bono in support of Irish Hospice Foundation, a national charity supporting those facing dying, death, and bereavement.

When we meet Peter, he's a young boy struggling to come to terms with the death of his mother. Upon hearing stories of a wolf on the loose, Peter decides to explore the vast meadow and forest nearby to try and find the wolf himself. Along the way, he encounters creatures who help him on his quest while contending with hunters who are aiming to capture the wolf.

The work of Irish Hospice Foundation echoes throughout the story with the dominant themes of love and loss. Death is an inevitable part of life, but it causes overwhelming fear and grief for many. The message of *Peter and the Wolf* is that no one need ever feel alone. There are other family members to turn to, like Grandfather. There are friends to rely on, like the bird, the duck, and the pussycat.

Even the unknown, which can seem so terrifying – from the deep, dark forest to the hungry wolf – turns out to be important and inspiring. By entering the forest and facing the wolf, Peter confronts his own sense of loss and grief, and finally begins to understand his own complex emotions.

Just like Peter, whatever you're going through, you're not alone. Irish Hospice Foundation gives care and support to anyone facing end of life or bereavement, and everyone taking care of them. Through education and services, including Nurses for Night Care and the Bereavement Support Line, Irish Hospice Foundation strives to ensure that every person can die and grieve well, whatever their age and wherever they are.

I'll be your
feathered friend.

We spin a traditional fairy tale into a unique adaptation that also incorporates the topic of loss, redemption, and recovery. It's my hope that this *Peter and the Wolf* becomes a balm for any child dealing with loss.

— Gavin Friday

I'll take you
under my wing!

DK | Penguin Random House

Adapted and Curated by
Gavin Friday and Alistair Norbury

Publisher Francesca Young
Senior Designer Elle Ward

Design Assistant Sif Nørskov
Senior Editor Marie Greenwood
Production Editor Becky Fallowfield
Senior Production Controller Ena Matagic
Publishing Director Sarah Larter

With thanks to Emma Hanson, Stephen McNally and the rest of the team at Blink Industries, and to Francesca Harper, Andrea Mills, Shawn Sarles, and Rebecca Smart

First published in Great Britain in 2023
by Dorling Kindersley Limited
DK, One Embassy Gardens, 8 Viaduct Gardens,
London, SW11 7BW

The authorised representative in the EEA is
Dorling Kindersley Verlag GmbH.
Arnulfstr. 124, 80636 Munich, Germany

A CIP catalogue record for this book
is available from the British Library.
ISBN: 978-0-2416-6773-6

Printed and bound in Slovakia

www.dk.com

MIX
Paper | Supporting
responsible forestry
FSC™ C018179

This book was made with Forest Stewardship Council™ certified paper – one small step in DK's commitment to a sustainable future. **For more information go to www.dk.com/our-green-pledge**

PETER AND THE WOLF: THE ANIMATED FILM

Created and developed by
Gavin Friday and Alistair Norbury

Directors Stephen McNally and Elliot Dear

Executive producers Bono, Gavin Friday, Alistair Norbury, Amy Friedman, Ollie Green, Kim Howitt, Benjamin Lole, Stuart Souter, James Stevenson Bretton
Producer Adriana Piasek-Wanski
Line Producer Patrick Brennecke
Production Manager Maryam Anibaba
Production Coordinator Lucy McPhail
Production Assistant Imogen Andrews
Production Accountant Anastasia Dickson
Accountant Amy Savvides

Original story adaptation by
Gavin Friday
Story development by
Sophie Heawood and Séamas O'Reilly
Additional dialogue edit by
Séamas O'Reilly and Gavin Friday
Additional story by Elliot Dear, Ben Lole, Stephen McNally

Head of Story Michael Schlingmann
Storyboard Artists Tim Dillnutt and Yoshimichi Tamura
Storyboard Clean-Up Artist Julia Helou

Editor Simon Bullen
Animation Editor Joseph Rowe
Assistant Editor Christina Conradi

Art Director Melissa Malone
Character Designer Julien Becquer
Concept Artists Isa Bancewicz, Marlène Beaube, Heidi Smith
Prop Designer Matthew Davies
Matte Painter Xavier Ren
Additional Illustrations
Jordan Hewson and Eve Hewson

Production Designer Emma-Rose Dade
Lead Model Maker Rachel Crook

Model makers Lorna Bailey, Areeya Bass, Connor Chung, Beattie Hartley, Kat Simpson, Robin Smith, Jade Spilhaus, Saskia Tomlinson
Scenic Artist Kaylie Joy Black
Painter James Wilkes
Carpenter James Moss
Art Department Trainee Maria Malone
Screenskills Animation Trainee
Chris Plimmer
Scene Build Artists Leroy Ayton and Ruben Berkeley O'Reilly

Animation Director Yoshimichi Tamura
2D Animation Supervisor Robert Milne
2D Animators Ludivine Berthouloux, Charles Bonifacio, Aude Carpentier, Giulio De Toma, Tim Dillnutt, Peter Dodd, Setareh Erfan, Daryl Graham, Freya Hotson, Reg Isaac, Andy McPherson, Alice Parkes, Michael Schlingmann, Andrea Simonti, Andreas Wessel-Therhorn
2D Background Character Animators
Leroy Aynton and Ruben Berkeley O'Reilly
2D Clean-Up Animation Supervisor
Eleonora Quario
Lead 2D Clean-up Animator
Jessica Leslau
2D Clean-Up Animators Alejandra Anguita, Alexandra Sasha Balan, Judit Boor, Harry Davidson, Charlotte Davis, Denise Dean, Angeline De Silva, Gerry Gallego, Alice Guzzo, Bianca Howell, Raquel Juan Maestre, Katerina Kremasioti, Lisa O'Sullivan, Alison Oxborrow, Iona Menzies, Kat Michaelides, Alice Parkes, Estefanía Romón Villalobos, Clara Schildhauer, Jack Sleeman, Jay Wren
Lead 2D Shadow Animator
Jamie-Lee Reynolds
2D Shadow Animators Ruben Berkeley O'Reilly, Joanna Boyle, Chrysoula Varia
Additional 2D Shadow Animator
Xavier Ren

Lead 2D FX Animator Andreu Campos
2D FX Animator Daniel Leyva

Compositing Supervisor Stephen McNally
Pre-Compositing Artist
Niamh Fitzmaurice
Compositing Artists Tim Bentley, Abigail Fairhurst, Corinne Ladeinde, Jesse Richards, Rob Ward

Additional Compositing Artist
Alasdair Brotherston

Screen Skills Compositing Trainee
Will Oyowe

Systems Engineers Christos Georgallides, Steve Harman, Chandeep Heera, Adam Kerrins, Ngandu Elric Tshimanga
Digital Intermediate provided by
Goldcrest Post Production
Digital Colourist Adam Glasman
Digital On-Line Editor Ellie Clissett
Digital Intermediate Producer
Lily Morgan
Head of Production Jonathan Collard
Head of Post Production Rob Farris
DI Technical Supervisor Lawrence Hook
DI Assistants Alfie McDonald and Isabelle Soole
Head of Extraction and Delivery
Tom Corbett

Special thanks to
Faye Purcell, Jennifer Pitcher, Emma Pactus, and Leah McCullagh.
Irish Hospice Foundation:
Marie Donnelly, Sharon Foley, Helen McVeigh, Paula O'Reilly, Kathy Gilfillan, Caroline Erskine
Irish Hospice Foundation is a registered charity in Ireland, registration number 20013554